Little Puffer Fish

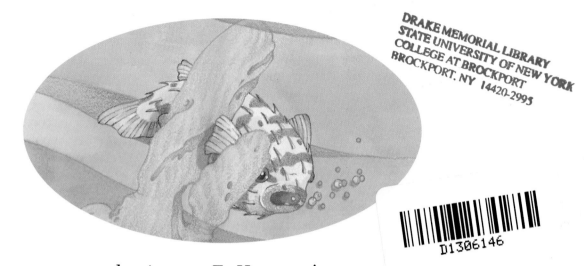

by Amany F. Hassanein

illustrations by Neesa Becker

Richard C. Owen Publishers, Inc.
Katonah, New York

The little puffer fish had spines all over his body.
He swam along the bottom of the sea.

Suddenly, a big fish appeared.

The big fish looked at the little puffer fish with hungry eyes and swam like an arrow toward him.

The little puffer fish darted here and there,
but there was no place to hide.

The little puffer fish
was so frightened that
he gulped water.

The more water he gulped,
the bigger he grew.

Soon he was so puffed up
that his sharp, pointy spines stuck out
all over his body.

The big fish stopped!
A puffed-up fish with sharp, pointy spines
is not good to eat.

And so, the big fish turned around
and swam away to search for
a different little fish to chase
and gobble up.